comets

Time Exchange

Jon Blake

Illustrated by
Clinton Banbury

CollinsEducational
An imprint of HarperCollinsPublishers

Published by Collins Educational
77-85 Fulham Palace Road, London W6 8JB

© HarperCollins*Publishers*

ISBN 0 00 323058 9

Illustration, page layout and cover illustration by Clinton Banbury.
Cover design by Clinton Banbury.

Commissioning Editor: Domenica de Rosa
Editor: Paula Hammond
Production: Susan Cashin

Typeset by Harper Phototypesetters Ltd, Northampton, England
Printed by Caledonian International, Glasgow, Scotland

Time Exchange

Contents

Chapter 1

Vive la France!

It was the time of the French exchange. Every year the school sent twenty pupils to invade France. Soon after, twenty French kids came over for their revenge. It was a wonderful way to promote world peace...

I put my name down to go. Then I blew my chances by letting off a stink bomb in the girls' toilets.

It wasn't the first time I'd done this kind of thing. Mr. Cole, my form teacher, said he had lost patience with me.

I am sending you to see Dr. Pike.

I went cold. Dr. Pike was the new school Counsellor. It was her job to talk to the nutters.

But there's nothing wrong with me!

That is for Dr. Pike to decide.

Dr. Pike was the weirdest person I had ever seen. Her skin had a faint blue tinge and her eyes never blinked. She made me lie on a couch while she went through pages of notes. She seemed to know everything about

This is the third time you've attacked the girls' toilets Rodney. Why?

'Cos I'm a nutter, Miss.

I am not a 'miss'. I am a doctor. And you are not a nutter. You are disturbed.

If you say so, Doctor.

Last month you blew up Kay Green's sports kit with a firework...

...The month before you put a live mouse in Sheryl Batten's lunch box. Tell me, Rodney, do you have a problem with girls?

It's them that's got the problem, Doctor.

Oh? Why's that?

They're only good for one thing.

And what is that?

Netball.

I laughed. Dr. Pike didn't. She made a few notes, then called Mr. Cole into the room.

"I'm recommending this boy for the exchange," she said.

Yes! France, here I come!

No Rodney. Not that exchange.

What other exchange is there?

Mr. Cole closed the door. Dr. Pike's voice dropped to a whisper.

The time exchange.

Time exchange?

Dr. Pike and Mr. Cole exchanged glances. "We're sending a pupil to the year 2055," explained Mr. Cole.

I checked my watch. No, it wasn't April 1st. And Mr. Cole was keeping a very straight face.

Chapter 2

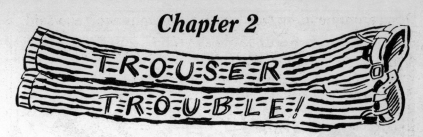

TROUSER TROUBLE!

Mum and Dad were very understanding when I told them I was going to the future. They helped me pack my case and told me not to hurry back on their account.

You never know. I might not come back at all!

Mum and Dad said nothing – just shared a little smile.

One week later the big day arrived. The French exchange kids were sent to the school gates and I was sent to the science lab. Dr. Pike was waiting with a man from the government and all my teachers. They took it in turns to shake my hand.

"Unlock the time trousers," ordered Dr. Pike.

"The what?" I spluttered.

Mr. Cole opened the stock room door, and there, amongst the Bunsen burners, was an old pair of brown cords with a plastic belt. Mr. Cole took them out and held them out towards me.

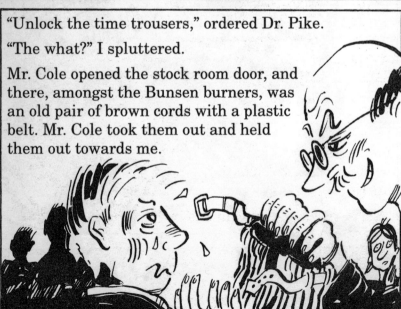

Put them on.

I'm not wearing them! Everyone'll laugh!

Not in 2055 they won't.

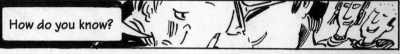

How do you know?

Dr. Pike made no reply. The teachers seized me while she pulled the revolting cords on to me and did up the belt.

AHHHHHHHEEEEEEE

Get the mirror.

Mr. Cole went back into the stock room and brought out a full-length mirror.

"No!" I cried. "I don't want to see!"

Look into the mirror, Rodney...

7

The mirror was right in front of me. I couldn't avoid it.

But the moment I caught sight of myself, there was a whooshing sound and tiny beads of light before my eyes. Then I hurtled down a whirling tunnel – just like the ones in those crap old sci-fi films. I saw images of birth, death and F.A. Cup replays. There was a massive gurgling noise and last night's supper came back to me.

Then everything went black.

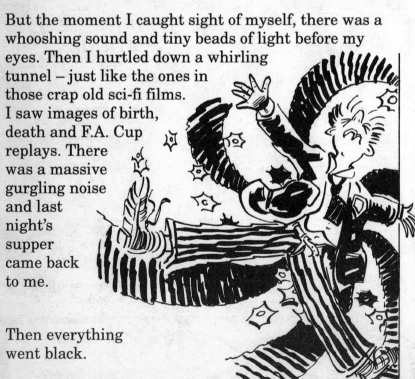

Chapter 3
Back to the Future

I came round to find two youths staring at me. Well, not staring at me, exactly. Staring at my trousers.

"Mm!" said the first.

"Mm!" said the second.

One was big and lumbering, with a slow sarcastic smile. The other was skinny and eager, with mean, weasel eyes.

"Err...is this...the future?" I asked cautiously.

The two youths dragged their eyes from my trousers and looked me in the face.

Karamba Karella.

Kanunga Kabeeba.

This was going to be difficult.

The two youths looked blank.

The two youths shrugged.
Then the big one pointed into
the distance.

"Kabang!" he barked, pushing me – hard – in the back.

We were on a huge wasteground, with nothing but rubble beneath our feet. The skinny one raced off across it, shooting at invisible enemies with an invisible gun. He was wearing the most ridiculous shoes, with heels the size of breeze blocks. No wonder he thought my brown cords were cool.

I strolled after the skinny lad, trying not to laugh. The big lad followed. If they were trying to make me nervous, they were doing a good job...

So. They don't speak English in 2055?

PTTHH

Kagana?

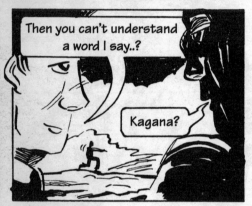

Then you can't understand a word I say..?

Kagana?

Your mate has got the stupidest shoes I've ever seen.

I turned my head and smiled broadly. The big lad smiled back.

TAKA TAKA TP

Only a total dickhead would wear shoes like that.

I smiled again. The big lad laughed a little.

We walked on. My feet tramped over a broken-down sign. On it, in faded paint, were the words FELLOWS HIGH SCHOOL. So this really was the future. And my old school was a pile of rubble! Something told me I would enjoy this time exchange.

We walked on for about a mile further. Then we came to a clearing. There was a circle of flagpoles with rotting animal heads stuck on the top. In the middle of these was a huge sign saying BOYS' TOWN. Beneath it was a hole. The skinny lad stopped there and pointed down.

I hope you don't think I'm going down there...

"Kabisha! Kabisha! Kabisha!" cried the skinny lad, stamping his feet impatiently. Only I wasn't really listening. Something had just occurred to me...

If you don't speak English...how come this place is called BOYS' TOWN?

The big lad looked at me. A little smile played upon his lips.

Who said we didn't speak English?

GULP!

Something told me I was in *big* trouble.

14

Oh! Come on! You didn't think I meant those things I said, did you? I was just joking...

Well, let's see what Arnie thinks about that, shall we?

The big lad called the skinny one over and asked me to repeat what I'd said about his shoes. The skinny one was *very* keen to hear this. He stood about a millimetre from my nose, staring me straight in the eyes.

I was just saying... fashions are different in 2055...

How?

Shoes are...taller...

SO!

Nothing... they're just different, that's all.

Arnie, if that was his name, marched on for a few
metres, then came back, breathing hard.

Were you laughing at me?

SNORT!

'Course not!

One more word about my
shoes...and you're dead.

Arnie drew a line across his
throat. I wasn't fazed.
At least, I didn't let him
see I was.

"Is your mate always like this?" I asked the big lad,
when Arnie had raced off again.

"Only since the accident," he replied.

I waited for the big lad to tell
me more about this accident.
He didn't.
"The name's
Sly," he said.
"Welcome to
the future."

Chapter 4

Big Girl's Blouse

It stank down the hole, and I soon found out why.
At the bottom was a huge barrack room with about
fifty lads in it. They were all lying around watching
action movies from the 1980s.

All of them wore shoes like Arnie's.

That was not a nice idea. The floor was solid granite. My nose would not enjoy it.

I don't think I can.

I knew it! He's a girl!

Well, I couldn't take that. I had to prove I was a man, even if it meant smashing my face to a pulp.

I held my breath, steeled myself, and dropped.

They caught me before I hit the ground.

Next second, the blindfold was off and I was looking into a sea of laughing faces.

"Put it there, Rod," said Sly, slapping palms.

"You're one of us, Rod," said Arnie, punching knuckles.

A warm feeling came over me. I liked Sly, and Arnie, and all the others who'd saved my face. They were good lads, every one of them.

So. What's next?

How about Jean-Claude van Damme in "Death Gut 23"?

Er...I was kind of hoping I'd meet some girls.

There was an uncomfortable silence.

You're sure about that?

Yeah! Why?

There was another uncomfortable silence. "O.K.," said Sly. "We'll go down to the youth arena."

Some of the others weren't so sure. Sly took me quietly to one side.

There's something you need to know...
The girls round here...They may not be your type...

What type are they?

They're big girls. If you see what I mean.

I winked. "Don't worry," I said. "That's just my type."

Chapter 5

TEAM TACTICS

There was no room for democracy in Boys' Town. Once Sly said we were going to the youth arena, that was that. Arnie acted as deputy, rounding up the lads who had gone to hide in the toilets.

"You're thinking like losers," said Sly. "We'd better have a team talk."

The lads sat with their heads bowed while Sly patrolled the room.

O.K. What's the first rule of chatting up girls?

Rule number two?

Don't let them dictate the game.

Keep it simple

What's rule number three?

Don't let them settle!!

Sly prowled around and started picking out individuals. After ten minutes of the team talk, they no longer looked like losers. But Sly wasn't finished yet.

How much are we going to give?

A hundred and ten per cent!!

ALL RIGHT!! Let's do it!

To a mighty roar, the lads funnelled up the stepladders and into the light. It was nice to know that, whatever else had changed, people still talked the same old football rubbish.

The youth arena was a deserted building in the centre of town. In fact, it was the only building in the centre of town. There was a bar on one side, which was closed, and a dance floor on the other. Two of the lads got some music going while the rest of us did some warm-ups.

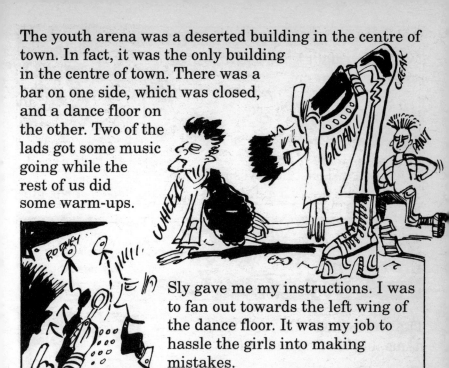

Sly gave me my instructions. I was to fan out towards the left wing of the dance floor. It was my job to hassle the girls into making mistakes.

Minutes passed. Arnie paced up and down, firing his make-believe gun.

Suddenly an engine drew up outside. The whole room was filled with an electric tension.

There were loud footsteps, and they were getting closer.

The door opened. My jaw dropped.
The girl who walked in was three metres tall.
The girls who followed her were even bigger.

To give him his dues, Sly stayed cool. He
walked straight up to the first girl
and pointed at me.

See my mate?
He fancies you.

The huge girl cast her eyes upon me.
I was terrified. With giant steps she bounded towards me.

It's him! He's the
one who
fancies you!

The girl turned to Arnie. "What's your
name, big boy?" she asked.

"Just call me the *luuve god*," said Arnie,
whose voice suddenly sounded like a
little tin whistle.

"Reckon you've got what it takes,
do you?" boomed the girl.

"I've got more than enough to satisfy you,"
peeped Arnie.

At this, the whole room was filled with a
mighty, terrifying noise. The big girls were
laughing. Arnie's would-be girlfriend patted
him gently on the head and walked back
to her mates.

I'm in with a
chance there.

24

Some of the girls stepped on to the dance floor. Sly made urgent gestures in my direction.

What are you playing at? Get stuck in there!

PUSH!

Nervously I stepped on to the dance floor and approached the nearest girl. She towered above me.

FANCY A DANCE?

I shouted up as loud as I could, but she couldn't hear me.

Suddenly I felt myself hoisted in the air, till I was level with the big girl's ear.

"Fancy a dance?" I repeated.

"I've got a dance," she replied.

I was lowered back to the floor and left with the handbags. I was relieved in a way. It wouldn't feel right, slow-dancing with my nose in a girl's belly-button.

Things didn't go any better for the others. Some tried smoking because it was supposed to make them look big. If it did, the girls didn't notice. They were wrapped up in a world of their own. Their conversation went right over our heads. All credit to the lads, they stuck in there. But it was a game of two halves – and we were losing them both.

Soon the frustration started to get to us. Fights broke out all over. When the time came for the last dance, there were hardly any lads still standing. Those that were had broken teeth and bleeding noses. The lights came up, the girls went home, and the lads looked round for some poor idiot to blame. I fitted the bill perfectly.

'Snot my fault. They were twice as big as us!

There was a shocked silence.

"Don't talk crap," said Arnie.

"What d'you mean?" I said.

"They're not *that* big," said Sly.

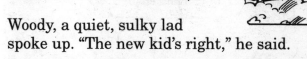

Woody, a quiet, sulky lad spoke up. "The new kid's right," he said.

"*And* they're getting bigger all the time," said Woody. "Soon we won't even be up to their knees."

Arnie walked right up close to me. It was the second time he'd done this, and his breath hadn't got any better.

This is traitors' talk...and you know what happens to traitors?

What's that then?

We send them back where they came from.

In a body bag!!!

The other lads laughed. Arnie swaggered out of the room, kicking a few chairs over as he went. I turned to Sly.

Does he often threaten to kill people?'

No. Usually he just does it.

Chapter 6

HeroTalk

I didn't sleep well that night. They'd given me the lumpiest bed in Boys' Town. Most of the lads stayed up till dawn watching movies, and when I went down for breakfast, all I found was Woody. I got the feeling he'd been waiting for me.

Bacon and eggs?

"Sure!" I said. It was the first time anyone had offered me anything to eat since I'd arrived.

Er... should bacon be blue?

All food is blue. Since the accident.

Ah.

Woody leaned across the table and lowered his voice. "You talk a lot of sense, Rod," he said.

"About what," I asked.

"About the girls," replied Woody.

"They're *massive,*" I said.

Woody shook his head sadly. "It was just over three years ago," he said. "The Ganuna B reactor in Australia went into meltdown. Burnt right through the Earth's core and came up in our playground."

"Wow!" I said.
"So how come you weren't killed?"

"We were lucky," said Woody. "They brought out this new drug. Prevented radiation sickness. But they never knew about the side-effects..."

"So the drug made the girls grow?" I asked.

"Not straight away," Woody replied. "It happened after the girls were sent off to live on their own – the government didn't want us mating and making two-headed babies."

I thought for a while.

Suddenly I felt hopeful.

I jumped to my feet. Woody pressed me down again. "Forget it," he said. "They won't let us near the place."

Woody's words fell on deaf ears. I'd seen my chance to become a hero.

Chapter 7
Big Ideas

That afternoon I took a fistful of radiation pills and set off on an old bike. The woods nearby were littered with paper plates and plastic forks dumped by the lads. On the other side of the woods were the most incredible fields, full of blue corn two metres high. I skirted around the field and came to a sign saying GIRLS' TOWN INDUSTRIAL ESTATE. It sounded grim, but it was nothing of the kind. The factories were made of glass and colourful tubes of metal. Inside, music pulsed while the girls worked confidently. I don't know why, but this made me feel smaller than ever. I thought about sneaking up and slinging a stink bomb inside, but the thought of getting caught sent me cold.

Past the factories, there were a group of domes with a lawn in front. On the lawn, girls were preparing a meal. I hid behind a tree and watched.

The first thing that struck me was the disgusting language the girls were using. All right, so boys swore all the time, but that was different.
The girls laughed and joked about things I wouldn't even write on a toilet wall. I had a strong feeling it ought to be stopped, but there was no-one to stop it, except me maybe.

After a while the girls from the fields and the factories arrived. Everyone sat down to lunch. Suddenly I noticed something which made my hopes rise. The girl at the far end was no taller than me!

33

The small girl didn't seem to fit in at all. She was awkward and shy. The others talked, excitedly, with their mouths full, but she didn't talk at all. It wasn't long before they noticed she was silent. The girl next to her tried to cheer her up.

That explained everything! The girl was on a time exchange too!

There was an awkward silence.

My heart leapt. But the big girls looked rather sorry for Tracy.

"We used to think like you," said one.

"We really thought we needed boys at first," said a second girl, "but after a while, we realised we preferred it this way."

"Boys take everything over," said a third.

"Boys crush anyone sensitive," said a fourth.

"Girls act stupid when boys are around," said a fifth.

Soon Tracy began to get angry.

There was a roar of laughter.
Suddenly Tracy leapt to her feet.

The laughter stopped.

Tracy's lip quivered.

Suddenly she burst into tears. The girl next to her put an arm round her shoulder. Tracy said that no-one had ever accepted her. Everyone thought she was stupid. Everyone thought she was ugly. Everyone thought she was fat.

Two of the big girls took Tracy indoors. By now she was sobbing like a baby. The other girls became very serious. Some didn't think they'd made Tracy welcome enough. Others said how difficult it was to come from another time sector. But they all agreed she had to learn.

Twenty minutes passed before Tracy came back out. She had stopped crying and looked much happier.

She was also half a metre taller.

Chapter 8
Cry Babies

I could hardly control myself when I got back to Boys' Town.

I've got it! I've got the secret!

What secret's this, Rodney?

HA HA HA HA HA!!

The lads laughed.

The secret of being a moron!

The secret of growing, actually.

I told the whole story.
My visit to Girls' Town, the small girl, how she had got upset, and how she grew before my eyes.

So what's the secret?

Isn't it obvious?

Go on.

Crying!

The lads looked at me with blank faces.

Is this your idea of a joke?

Why should I make a joke like that?

Arnie sneered. "No-one's making me cry!"

Sly hushed him. "Cool it, Arnie," he said. "Let's give the guy a chance."

So, how are we going to go about this crying thing then?

Arnie looked blank.

But Sly kept his cool. "Let's do as the man says," he said.

The plan went into action. The lads fetched old videophone records, toys and faded photos. We sat in a circle and put them down in front of us. Then we started trying to feel something.

It wasn't easy. Ten minutes passed, and not a single tear.

All credit to Sly, however. As usual, he was prepared to give a lead.

He sat perfectly still, with his eyes fixed on a photo of his old dog. For a long time he showed no emotion, Then, with a deadly serious face, he turned to me.

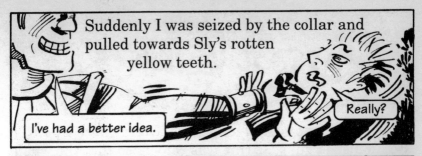

Suddenly I was seized by the collar and pulled towards Sly's rotten yellow teeth.

I've had a better idea.

Really?

We'll beat the shit out of you. Then you'll cry all right.

I began to produce a certain amount of liquid, but it wasn't tears.

Sly rolled up his sleeve. "Ready, Rodney?" he said. My brain raced, then suddenly I had it.

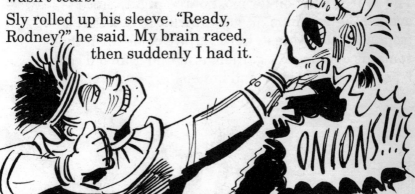

ONIONS!!!!

The only problem was that none of the lads had ever heard of onions. All their meals arrived in packets, and included nothing but meat. I had to explain what an onion was and how, if you chopped them, they made you cry.

O.K., Rodney. But this is your last chance.

Last chance before what?

Sly turned to Arnie. Arnie rubbed his hands together gleefully.

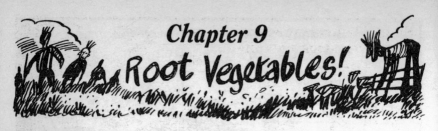

Chapter 9

Root Vegetables!

I didn't enjoy the search for onions. Everywhere I went, I had an armed guard. Arnie was convinced that the whole thing was a trick and I was about to make a run for it. They even made me swap trousers with Rutsy so I couldn't zip off back to the past. Unfortunately Rutsy hadn't washed his trousers for three years. They were so stiff I could hardly bend my knees.

The search went on for most of the night. Since everything was blue, it was difficult to tell a beetroot from a potato. At last, however, we came upon the remains of a market garden, and under an old cold frame, we found six small onions.

Suddenly Arnie produced a large and savage-looking knife

W-what's that for?

Right...

The onions, of course.

Ah! Of course!

I held out my hand. "Shall I be mother?" I said.

Keeping his eyes fixed on mine, Arnie handed me the knife.

O.K. Gather round everybody.

The lads gathered round. I placed an onion on a flat stone and began to act like Mrs. Frost, our domestic science teacher.

First, we chop the onion...

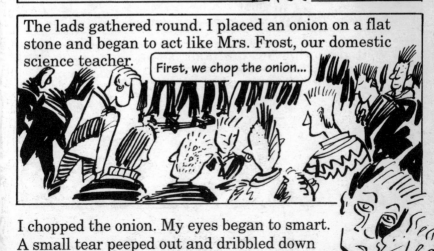

I chopped the onion. My eyes began to smart. A small tear peeped out and dribbled down my cheek. The lads were duly impressed.

CHOP CHOP

43

The lads crowded in close, desperate for a sniff. I chopped busily. First one, then another began to weep.

Soon the lads were fighting with each other to get the biggest sniff. Tears flowed like rain.

The excitement was intense. Who would be the first to show signs of growth? A minute passed. Then another. Then another.

We waited another few minutes. No-one grew a single millimetre.

I soon got an answer to this question. Two lads seized me by the arms and, with war-like chants, marched me back towards Boys' Town, and certain doom.

Chapter 10
The Pits

They put me in a place called the pit. They gave me blue bread and water and left me to sweat. Up above I could hear urgent conversation. They were discussing how to kill me.

"We could give him the Chinese death of a thousand cuts," said Rutsy.

"Or drown him in the septic tank," said Sly.

"Let's just hunt him like a pig," said Arnie.

There was vote on the matter. Arnie's suggestion won. Arnie, after all, was the expert when it came to killing. Besides, a hunt gave all the lads the chance to get involved. It was good sport and fair on everyone – except me, of course. My chances of survival were zero.

Believe me, when you're facing the end, you think fast. When they came for me I had my plan all worked out.

"You're supposed to give me a last request," I said.

The lads discussed this.

"O.K.," said Sly. "Last request. Fire away."

I want to die in my own trousers.

Arnie laughed.

You'll be doing something in your own trousers, that's for sure.

Rutsy's face dropped.

That's a point... Better do as he says.

Are you mad? He'll be straight back to his own time!

Not without a mirror.

The lads were ordered to hide all the mirrors. I climbed out of Rutsy's trousers and stood them against the wall. Half a minute later I was back in those repulsive brown cords. I was starting to almost like them.

It was a fresh, clear day as they led me to the edge of the woods. The world looked beautiful. I certainly wasn't ready to leave it.

Rodney, you will *go* on my first whistle. Lads, you will *go* on my *second* whistle.

PEEEEP!!

I got into sprint position. The lads stood directly behind me, each armed with an old school javelin. Sly's whistle went. I was off like a bullet. Only one thing was in my mind: I must get to Girls' Town.

I remember little of the chase. But I do remember my first sight of the girls' domes, like an oasis in the desert. Hardly daring to look behind, I raced straight out across the lawn.

But the girls were ready for me. They spread out across the lawn to block my path. It was like facing a karate formation dancing team. The lads behind obviously saw what was happening because the footsteps stopped and the war-cries died out.

Get back now!

No boys! That's the rule!

I pulled my most pathetic little-boy face. "But they're going to kill me!" I whimpered.

To my horror, not one girl was moved.

"That," said the dreadlock girl, "is your business."

This time I felt a real tear brimming.

What about your maternal instincts?

Ha! Ha! Twentieth-century rubbish!

"We don't have to be mothers," said a second.

"We'll be what we want to be," said a third.

At this I overflowed. Real tears began to stream down my cheeks. "I want to go home!" I cried.

Your home is Boys' Town.

No it isn't! It's 26, Gardenia Court, in the twentieth century!

The thought of my home finished me off completely. I began to shudder and sob like a baby. It was a weird sensation. Nature was taking me over.

Through a bleary mist I saw the girls in conversation, I heard the words "time exchange". They were discussing if I should be treated differently.

The discussion ended. A second girl stepped forward. She was four metres tall, super-confident, and her name was Tracy.

Tell us, how did you treat girls in your own time?

Be honest! Be honest, or it's back to Boys' Town!

Very well indeed.

I hung my head.

"How did you treat girls in your own time?" Tracy repeated.

"Like objects," I mumbled.

I don't know why it occurred to me to say this. But the moment I said it, I realised it was true. And speaking the truth seemed to open a tap. All kinds of other things came flooding out. I even said I was scared of girls, which really did sound stupid, but was true all the same.

SNIFF!!

Tracy turned to the other girls.

He's telling the truth.

Are you sure?

Yes. I go to his school.

I looked at Tracy with amazement. She was obviously one of the quiet girls at school. The ones you never notice.

The girls held another discussion, then invited me inside.

Chapter 11

Girls' Talk

It is hard to describe what happened inside the girls'
dome. The tears stopped but the talking carried on. The
more I talked, the more I wanted to talk. I confessed to
everything. Then it was my turn to listen. The girls told
their stories and spared no detail. They made me
understand things I'd never even thought about. I felt
strangely involved in their lives, almost as if they were
my own. I fumed when they told an angry story. I
laughed when they told a funny story. I squirmed when
they told an embarrassing story.

I don't think I'd ever felt more relaxed.

Before I knew it, I was fast asleep.

I don't know how long I slept. I half-remember being carried, but it was difficult to tell if it was a dream. Then I half-woke and realised I was in a little summer house in the garden. It was perfect. And then, like a nightmare returning...

The windows shattered. The room was full of bodies, gruff voices, devilish masks and glinting knives. The lads had come for me.

In a blind panic, I leapt out of bed. Then something unreal happened.

The lads began to back away.

I suddenly realised I was looking down on the tops of their heads.

Somehow, I had become the first Big Boy.

You were saying, Arnie?

In a mad scramble, the lads fought their way out of the door and legged it. Moments later, the girls arrived. They seemed to be as gobsmacked as the lads.

"It's impossible," said one.

"He must have reached E-factor," said a second.

"Boys can't reach E-factor!" said the third.

There was a moment's silence.

The three girls looked me hard in the eyes. "What are we feeling?" they asked. I looked at them, really looked at them, the way babies look at people.

"You're feeling puzzled," I replied, "but deep inside, you're also feeling relieved."

And what are you feeling?

Exactly the same.

They laughed. We all laughed. "That's it," they said. "He's reached E-factor."

Chapter 12
No Place Like Home

It was the fear that did it. It was the fear that broke down my defences. Once I felt for the girls, really felt for them, up I went. Now the fear was gone, and I was as high as a kite.

You might think that all my trials were over. But I had one big problem left. I stared sadly at the time trousers and wondered how I could ever get them on again. I needed to be able to wear them if I was ever going to get home again.

The girls all sat round and pondered. In Girls' Town, if one person had a problem, everybody had a problem.

I considered this for a while, but it was no good.

The other girls stamped on this straight away. It simply wasn't allowed.

We pondered another few minutes, but were lost for ideas.

You could always stay.

No. Thanks, but I want to see my mum.

Of course. Well, I'm afraid we're going to have to leave you with it. It's time for our swimming and exercise session.

I understand.

O.K., girls. Time to get into our swimwear.

A few minutes later, the girls were changed and ready for swimming – and lo and behold, the time trousers now fitted me perfectly!

Nothing had changed while I'd been away. Exactly the same crowd was there to greet me in the science lab.

Dr. Pike gazed at me eagerly.

So, Rodney. Do you think you benefited from your holiday?

It was...a bit of a shock.

In what way?

Such different food.

The teachers noted this down, but Dr. Pike knew I was having her on. There was a strange bond between us, something I couldn't explain. I found it difficult to stop looking at her. She looked different, or maybe I'd never really seen her before.

Without further ado, Dr. Pike climbed into the time trousers, turned to the mirror, and was gone.